Franklin's Blanket

P9-CAB-894

No part of this publication may be reproduced in whole or in part, or stored in a retrieval system, or transmitted in any form, or by any means, electronic, mechanical, photocopying, recording or otherwise, without written permission of the publisher. For information regarding permission, write to Kids Can Press Ltd., 29 Birch Avenue, Toronto, Ontario M4V 1E2.

ISBN 0-590-25468-5

Text copyright © 1995 by Paulette Bourgeois
Illustrations copyright © 1995 by Brenda Clark
All rights reserved.
Published by Scholastic Inc.,
555 Broadway, New York, NY 10012,
by arrangement with Kids Can Press Ltd.
Interior illustrations prepared with
the assistance of Muriel Hughes Wood.

12 11 10 9 8 7 6 5 4   6 7 8 9/9 0/0

Printed in the U.S.A.   23

First Scholastic printing, November 1995

Franklin's Blanket

Paulette Bourgeois
Brenda Clark

Scholastic Inc.
New York   Toronto   London   Auckland   Sydney

FRANKLIN could slide down a riverbank all by himself. He could count by twos and tie his shoes. He could even sleep alone — as long as he had a good-night story, a good-night hug, a glass of water, a night-light, and his blue blanket.

In the beginning, the blanket was big and soft and edged in satin. But with all the snuggling and cuddling, it now had holes in the middle and tatters along the edges. Every year as Franklin got bigger, his blue blanket got smaller.

Franklin usually kept his blanket folded in his top drawer. One night, it wasn't there. Franklin searched around his room. He rummaged through his toy chest. He took everything out of his drawers and his books off the shelves. But he could not find his blue blanket anywhere.

He ran to tell his parents.

"Go back to bed," they said as soon as they saw him.

"But, but . . ." said Franklin.

"No buts," said Franklin's father. "You have had a good-night story, a good-night hug, two glasses of water, and I turned on your night-light myself."

"But I can't find my blanket," said Franklin.

So Franklin and his parents hunted everywhere.
"Try to remember," said Franklin's mother. "When did you last have it?"

Franklin thought.

In the morning, after a fight with Bear, Franklin had snuggled with the blanket until he felt better.

In the afternoon, when thunder crashed and lightning flashed, Franklin had covered himself with the blanket until all was calm.

He was sure that after the storm he had put the blanket back where it belonged.

When Franklin and his parents looked, the blanket wasn't there.

"We'll find it tomorrow," said Franklin's mother.

"I can't sleep without my blanket," said Franklin.

"I have an idea," said Franklin's father. He left the room and came back with an old, yellow blanket.

"What's that?" asked Franklin.

"It was mine," said Franklin's father. "Maybe it will make you feel better."

Franklin tried to snuggle the old, yellow blanket, but it wasn't the same. He missed his own blanket terribly, and it took Franklin a long, long time to fall asleep.

The next morning, Franklin began a search for his blanket. He went to Bear's house first. He looked so glum that Bear asked, "What's wrong, Franklin? Did your mother give you brussels sprouts again?"

"Worse," said Franklin. "I can't find my blanket."

"It's not here," said Bear. "Besides, my mother says big bears like me are too old for baby blankets. Maybe you don't need a blanket."

Franklin knew that Bear always slept with his stuffed bunny. "What about your bunny?" asked Franklin.

"Bunnies are different," said Bear.

Next he tried Fox's house. The blanket wasn't there, either.

"Why don't we play?" asked Fox.

"No," said Franklin. "I want to find my blanket."

"My father says worn-out blankets are no good to anybody," said Fox. "Maybe you should get a new blanket. I did."

"I like my old blanket," said Franklin.

Then Franklin went to Beaver's house. The blanket wasn't there. Franklin looked so sad that Beaver said, "You can borrow my Teddy until you find your blanket."

"Thank you, Beaver," said Franklin, holding Teddy tightly.

That night when Franklin went to bed, he had his father's yellow blanket and Beaver's Teddy. But it wasn't the same as sleeping with his own blue blanket.

At breakfast, Franklin's father sniffed and pinched his nose. "Do you smell something odd?" he asked. "A sort of musty, old-sock smell?"

Franklin and his mother sniffed, too.

Then Franklin remembered. "I think I know what smells," he said.

Franklin reached under his chair and pulled out his blue blanket. *Plop!* A handful of cold, slimy brussels sprouts spilled out of the blanket and onto the floor.

His mother and father stared with amazement.

"Look!" said Franklin. "I found my blanket. I forgot I put it here."

"You forgot to eat your brussels sprouts, too," said Franklin's mother.

"Whoops," said Franklin, looking a little sheepish.

"Old, cold brussels sprouts sure do stink," said Franklin's father.

"All brussels sprouts stink," said Franklin.

Franklin's mother smiled. "I used to hate cabbage," she said. "Now *that's* a stinky vegetable."

"Asparagus!" said Franklin's father. "That's even stinkier than brussels sprouts and cabbage mixed together."

"Broccoli!" shouted Franklin. Then he stopped. He liked broccoli. "It stinks, but I wouldn't hide broccoli," he said.

"That's good news," said his father.

Franklin helped to tidy the mess.

Then Franklin picked up his blanket.
"I don't care that you are old and full of holes,"
he said. "But you sure do need a bath."

That night, before his good-night story, his good-night hug, and a glass of water, Franklin put his father's yellow blanket back where it belonged. He was glad he lived in a house where even old blankets had their special place.